ESSENTIAL FITNESS

STRETCHING & BALANCE

BY REBECCA MORRIS

An Imprint of Abdo Publishing
abdobooks.com

ABDOBOOKS.COM

Published by Abdo Publishing, a division of ABDO, PO Box 398166, Minneapolis, Minnesota 55439.

Printed in the United States of America, North Mankato, Minnesota.
052024
092024

Cover Photo: Shutterstock Images
Interior Photos: Mladen Mitrinovic/Shutterstock Images, 3, 18–19; Carlos Barquero/Shutterstock Images, 4–5; Shutterstock Images, 7, 9, 10, 15, 16–17, 25, 26, 30–31, 33, 43, 44–45, 47, 48, 52, 53, 60–61, 64, 67, 72, 73, 74–75, 79, 80, 84, 101; Andrey Popov/Shutterstock Images, 17; Chen Wenxian/Xinhua News Agency/Getty Images, 21; Rich Schultz/Getty Images Sport/Getty Images, 22; iStockphoto, 29, 39, 40, 55, 63, 81, 86, 98, 99; Dragon Images/Shutterstock Images, 36; Omar Vega/Getty Images Sport/Getty Images, 37; SDI Productions/iStockphoto, 50; Ryan J. Lane/iStockphoto, 59; Ankit Sah/iStockphoto, 68; Kino Masterskaya/Shutterstock Images, 70; Baza Production/Shutterstock Images, 87; Rich Legg/iStockphoto, 88–89; R. Farrarons/iStockphoto, 91; Joshua Rainey Photography/Bigstock, 92; StoryTime Studio/Shutterstock Images, 95; Amber N. Ford/iStockphoto, 100

Editors: Charlie Beattie and Christa Kelly
Series Designer: Jake Slavik

Library of Congress Control Number: 2023949422

PUBLISHER'S CATALOGING-IN-PUBLICATION DATA

Names: Morris, Rebecca, author.
Title: Stretching & balance / by Rebecca Morris
Description: Minneapolis, Minnesota: Abdo Publishing, 2025 | Series: Essential fitness | Includes online resources and index.
Identifiers: ISBN 9781098293314 (lib. bdg.) | ISBN 9798384912583 (ebook)
Subjects: LCSH: Stretching exercises--Juvenile literature. | Stretch (Physiology)--Juvenile literature. | Exercise therapy--Juvenile literature. | Physical fitness--Juvenile literature. | Exercise--Juvenile literature.
Classification: DDC 613.71--dc23

CONTENTS

STRETCHING AND DESTRESSING

CJ dropped his backpack and guitar case on the floor in his bedroom. He sighed and rubbed his neck. His whole body was feeling sore and stiff. He'd spent the day at school, sitting at an uncomfortable desk. Then, he'd gone to band practice and spent hours leaning over sheet music. Once practice was over, he'd headed to the library where he'd sat for another hour while typing an essay. The muscles in his back were tight and aching. He rolled his tense shoulders.

His gym teacher had mentioned that stretching could help ease back pain. CJ didn't consider himself an athlete. The only time he did stretches was when he was in gym class. He pulled out his

Sitting for long periods can cause undue stress on the back.

phone and downloaded the fitness app that his gym teacher had recommended. Maybe there was something on the app about stretches that might help him.

The app had dozens of free videos and articles. CJ clicked on a video titled "Guided Stretches." An instructor appeared on the screen. She was standing next to a rolled-up exercise mat.

"Hi there!" the woman smiled. "I'm your instructor, Brianna. Today, we'll be doing a 15-minute stretch routine for stiff shoulders and backs. This routine is easy to do anywhere, even in your living room or bedroom."

Brianna adjusted her stance so she was standing with her feet shoulder-width apart. CJ mirrored her movements. "We're going to begin with some dynamic stretches," she said. "It's good to warm up the muscles before holding longer stretches. As you follow the exercises, make sure your movements are fluid and controlled. Try not to move in fast, jerky motions."

Brianna started the workout by swinging her arms in front of her body. As she moved, she explained what she was doing and offered tips. CJ followed her instructions. He swung his arms in front of him, then let them swing behind his back. As he stretched, he felt the muscles in his shoulders and upper back loosening. Slowly, the ache in his back dulled, and the swings became easier and smoother.

Daily stretching can increase blood flow and help the body move through its full ranges of motion.

After 15 swings, Brianna moved on to neck rolls. She dipped her chin and slowly rotated her head toward her left shoulder. "This is another controlled motion," Brianna said. "We take seven seconds to roll our neck from one side to the other. Then we take a short pause and roll the other way."

"Now, take a quick break to check your posture. Make sure you're still standing straight, with your feet pointed forward and shoulder-width apart." CJ straightened his spine. He hadn't noticed that his posture had started to sag. "Also pay attention to how your weight is distributed. You should have an equal amount of weight on each foot."

FINDING RELIABLE VIDEOS ONLINE

There are many apps, videos, blogs, and websites with fitness information. Experts emphasize the importance of making sure a source's information is credible. Credible information comes from trained professionals with degrees, professional certifications, and work experience. Their background should be in physical therapy, exercise science, kinesiology, athletic training, or similar fields. To check if the content creators are reliable professionals, read the "About" section of the source. Credible sources also use current research to support their content, and they update the content regularly to ensure it is accurate.

CJ shifted his feet. Suddenly, he felt a bit more balanced. He copied Brianna's posture as she demonstrated standing with even shoulders and hips.

CJ followed along as Brianna did two more neck rolls. The rolls felt more natural with his adjusted posture. He checked his posture again as Brianna explained their next stretch. They were doing shoulder rolls. Brianna brought her shoulders up to her ears, then pushed her shoulders back in a circular motion. "As you're doing this exercise," Brianna instructed, "make sure your arms stay relaxed at your sides."

CJ repeated the exercise five times. After a short break, Brianna switched directions, rotating her shoulders up and forward. CJ followed along.

The exercises went by quickly. Brianna led him through arm circles, a side bend stretch, and a torso rotation stretch. He followed along, occasionally backing the video up to make sure he was doing the stretches correctly. He was surprised by how good his muscles felt. He'd expected stretching to be boring, but he felt energized.

"Nice job," Brianna said when they had finished. "That takes care of our dynamic stretching warm-up. Now we are going to hold some longer static stretches. These lengthen our muscles and help with flexibility."

Their first static stretch was a trapezius stretch. Brianna explained, "The trapezius is a muscle shaped almost like a diamond. It reaches from our lower neck to our shoulders

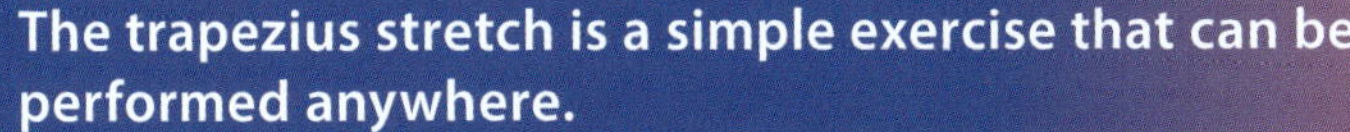

The trapezius stretch is a simple exercise that can be performed anywhere.

and down to our mid back. When the trapezius muscles are tight, our necks and upper shoulders feel tense."

CJ rubbed his neck again. That is definitely how his neck and shoulders were feeling. He followed Brianna's movements as she stood tall and raised her arm. "Keeping your shoulder down, lift your right arm over your head and place your hand just above your left ear. Now, look straight ahead, and tilt your neck to your

The back has three layers of muscles—the superficial layer, the intermediate layer, and the deep layer.

right shoulder." CJ felt the muscles in his neck stretch. "Be very gentle," Brianna said. "Push just enough that you can feel a stretch. Overstretching can strain or damage our muscles. Pay attention to how your body feels. Stretching should never feel sharp or painful."

ANIMAL STRETCHES

Humans aren't the only animals that stretch. Many animals move in ways that look like stretching. This is a normal part of animal behavior called pandiculation. This behavior occurs after sleep or rest. Researchers believe these movements awaken the muscles and brain. Several stretch and balance exercises are named after animal pandiculations. These exercises include cat, camel, pigeon, and butterfly stretches.

As CJ stretched, Brianna reminded viewers to take deep, steady breaths. "It's common for us to hold our breath without knowing it, especially when we're stretching," Brianna said, "but it's important to keep breathing. Holding our breath makes our muscles tighter."

CJ concentrated on his breathing. Each time he exhaled, the stretch seemed to get deeper. As he breathed, he felt his arms relax.

After 30 seconds on each side, Brianna announced that they'd be moving on to a scapulae stretch. She placed her right hand on the back of her head and gently turned her head until she was looking down at her right armpit. CJ copied the motion. He felt the exercise stretching his back, shoulders, and the side of his neck. After 30 seconds,

Brianna repeated the stretch with her other arm. CJ placed his left arm on the back of his head. The stretch felt a lot stronger on this side.

"It's normal for one side of the body to feel tighter than the other side," Brianna said. "Stretches like this will help loosen those muscles."

After another 30 seconds, Brianna led him through a triceps stretch followed by a stretch for the posterior shoulder capsule. "Posterior means the back of the shoulder," Brianna explained. She stretched her right arm across her body. With her other hand, she gently pressed her right elbow to push her arm further toward her body. CJ did the same and felt a stretch in the back of his shoulder. It felt like the muscles were getting longer.

"Let's do one more before we go onto our mats," Brianna said. "This stretch opens the chest. Clasp your

EXERCISE MATS

There are many different kinds of exercise mats. Experts recommend different mats for different exercise goals. For stretching and balance, mats should be a few inches longer than a person's height. Experts suggest mats with good grip for stretching exercises. These mats are made of materials such as cork, rubber, or PVC. These materials prevent sliding. Mats come in a range of thicknesses from just 0.16 inches (0.4 cm) thick to one inch (2.5 cm) thick or more.[1] Thicker mats add more cushion for the body, but they make balance harder.

hands behind your back and squeeze your shoulder blades together." She had her hands interlaced by the base of her spine. "This stretch is great for people who spend a lot of time sitting at a computer or looking down at a book or a screen. When we're sitting or looking down, we usually slouch forward and round our shoulders. This stretch pulls our shoulders back." CJ copied her movements. He felt some of the tension leaving his shoulders.

"Good job!" Brianna said. "Now let's unroll our mats. We're going to start with bird dogs." CJ paused the video. After a few minutes of rummaging through his basement closet, he found his mom's old yoga mat. He brought it to his room and laid it on the floor. He propped his phone up on a shoebox and unpaused the video. "Bird dogs are both a stretch and a balance exercise," Brianna explained. "They'll also help you work your core muscles."

Brianna unrolled her mat and knelt down. She placed her palms on the mat. "Place your hands and knees on the mat," she said. "Keep your hands in line with your shoulders, maintaining a small bend in your elbows. Keep your knees in line with your hips. Then, lift your left arm and your right leg, keeping them straight and parallel to the floor. Use your core to keep your back straight. We don't want our backs and necks to dip down, arch up, or rotate open."

CJ copied the slow movement. He wobbled as he raised his limbs. Brianna held the position and then slowly lowered her limbs back to their starting position. Then, she repeated with the opposite limbs. "Draw your stomach muscles in to engage them and help with balance," Brianna advised. "Squeezing the glutes when you lift your limbs is another way to stay stable."

CJ wobbled during the first few repetitions. He even had to put his hand down once to keep from falling over. He focused on squeezing his glutes and the muscles in his stomach. Slowly, the repetitions began to feel easier.

"Great work!" Brianna said. "Now try to stretch your limbs out even farther. Really extend like someone is pulling your hand forward and your foot backward," she said. CJ did. It seemed like his body was getting longer, almost as if he were growing an inch or two taller.

Brianna led them through ten repetitions, holding the position for about ten seconds each time. After a short break, they did a second set. By the last few reps, CJ found that he could hold his limbs up without wobbling.

"Nice job!" Brianna said after another two balance exercises. "Let's end with the child's pose stretch. Kneel on the mat and rest your hips on your heels. Then, lean forward until your forehead is touching the mat. Now, stretch your arms straight out in front of you with your palms flat on the mat." CJ followed her instructions.

Bird dogs aid with body stability by working the muscles in the back, core, and glutes.

They held the pose for an entire minute. He felt the stretch in his neck, shoulders, back, hips, and even ankles.

"That's all for our workout today!" Brianna said. "Remember, there are other videos with lower body and total body stretching routines, seated stretches, core work, and balance challenges. Try a variety of workouts to build regular stretching and balance exercises into your weekly schedule. Have a great day!"

CJ felt good as he rolled up his mat. His back and neck were looser than they'd been in days. He rolled his shoulders. The ache was nearly gone. He felt like he was standing taller and straighter than he had been before the workout. Before CJ closed the app, he marked the routine as one of his favorites, and he picked out another one to try the next day.

VIRTUAL CLASSES AND APPS

Virtual classes and fitness apps grew more popular during the COVID-19 pandemic that began in 2020. A 2022 article from National Public Radio reported, "At the height of the pandemic, when going to the gym wasn't an option, millions of people began exploring virtual workouts from home for the first time."[2]

Virtual classes and app technology offer people stretching and balance programs they can complete anywhere and at any time. Virtual classes can be live streamed or prerecorded to watch on demand. There are a variety of offerings. Apps may include videos, illustrations, detailed descriptions, and voice-guided directions.

Virtual stretching and balance apps may also have features such as challenges, calendars for tracking

Some families or groups work out together at home using virtual classes.

progress, and reminders that encourage users to practice stretching and balance regularly. Some platforms also come with social media channels or other ways of interacting with fellow users and fitness professionals.

Fitness technology such as apps and online classes can be accessible, affordable, motivating, and easy to incorporate into everyday life. They also introduce users to new kinds of exercise and allow them to tailor routines to their schedules and goals. However, one drawback of this kind of technology is that prerecorded videos do not allow for feedback from instructors or personalized guidance. Still, researchers believe that this technology will continue to affect how people integrate stretching, balance, and other kinds of exercise into their lives.

CHAPTER TWO

WHAT IS STRETCHING AND BALANCE?

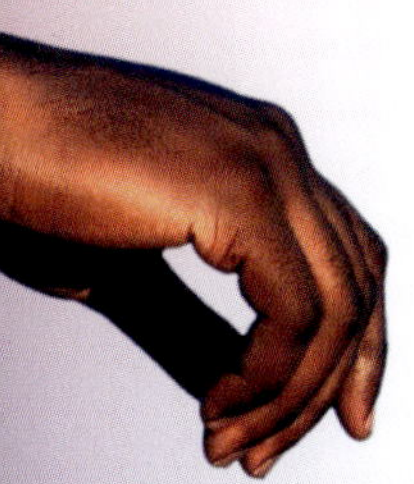

Stretching and balance exercises can help maintain a healthy body. They are used as part of general health and wellness programs for people of all ages. Athletes incorporate them as techniques to support injury prevention, performance, and recovery.

People with chronic health conditions also use these exercises to help manage symptoms. Older adults incorporate stretching and balance routines to prevent injury. They are particularly effective in reducing the risk of falls. Stretching and balance exercises are versatile. People can integrate them into their daily lives at home, in gyms, or even on vacation.

How someone benefits from stretching often depends on their overall health and fitness goals.

HISTORY OF STRETCHING AND BALANCE

People have practiced stretching and balance exercises for thousands of years. Some researchers believe these practices have prehistoric origins. Ancient stretching and balance practices have roots in yoga, martial arts, and both athletic and military training.

Yoga developed in India around 3,000 BCE in the Indus-Sarasvati civilization. The practice incorporated breathing, meditation, and postures to connect the body, mind, and spirit. From about 2600 BCE onward, people did breathing exercises. Yoga practices emerged that combined breathing and posture exercises. Stretches based on animal behavior also developed. These practices were believed to cure and prevent illness.

Martial arts gradually developed over thousands of years in many ancient cultures, including in Mongolia, China, Japan, and India. Researchers believe martial arts evolved from war dances and early forms of self-defense. Many martial arts practices require flexibility. Some styles, such as Tai Chi, emphasize balance and slow, fluid movement. Experts today still recommend practices such as Tai Chi to improve balance.

Stretching and balance training were used in ancient times to prepare athletes for competitions. They were also used to ready soldiers for combat. This practice of using stretching and balance training to

Tai Chi developed as a martial art in China. It has been described as meditation in motion.

prepare soldiers continues to modern times. A US Army training manual from 1946 includes stretches in its recommended warm-up drills. In addition, the manual emphasizes balance and suggests tumbling exercises to improve balance. David Behm, a professor who studies exercise physiology, believes stretching evolved alongside several organized team sports that developed in the 1800s and grew popular in the 1900s. These sports included ice hockey, baseball, basketball, volleyball, and football.

Several stretching styles emerged in the 1900s. In the 1950s and the early 1960s, ballistic stretching was a trend. Ballistic stretching involves jerky, bouncing motions to

Up to an hour before a game starts, athletes often take the field to stretch.

deepen a stretch. An example is performing a standing or seated toe touch and then rocking quickly and repeatedly to extend the range of motion. However, research emerged that indicated ballistic stretching could increase the risk of injury due to its forceful movements.

In the 1960s, static stretching became more common than ballistic stretching. Static stretching involves extending a muscle until there is a feeling of tension and then holding that position, typically for 15 to 60 seconds.[1] The tension in static stretching feels like a gentle pull, not like force or pain. For several decades, static stretching was common for general fitness and flexibility as well as for athletic warm-ups.

Experts began to reconsider static stretching in the 1990s and 2000s when new research suggested that static stretching before athletic activity could negatively affect performance. The research indicated that static stretching to reduce tension before athletic activity decreased response time and maximal strength in muscles. Dynamic stretching then became a more common way to warm up before athletic competition. Dynamic stretching involves fluid and controlled motions such as gentle arm and leg swings.

Balance training also began to shift in the 1990s and early 2000s to emphasize

STRETCHING INNOVATION

Proprioceptive neuromuscular facilitation (PNF) stretching developed in the 1940s and 1950s. Dr. Herman Kabat and physical therapists Dorothy Voss and Maggie Knott developed the technique. It is an alternative therapy to help patients recover their movement abilities after strokes and other illnesses. PNF stretching involves stretching a relaxed muscle for several seconds, contracting the muscle with resistance from a therapist, and then relaxing and stretching the muscle again. PNF stretching grew popular in the 1970s and is still used today. However, experts recommend this type of stretching only under the guidance of a physical therapist or certified athletic trainer because it is a complex technique. When incorrectly performed, it can cause injury.

dynamic movement. Static balance involves remaining still, such as standing on one leg for a set time. On the other hand, dynamic balance training draws from the movements of everyday life and sports skills. These are called functional movements. They include bending, reaching, moving side to side, and shifting body weight or weighted objects.

During this time, balance training also incorporated new equipment, including surfaces that are unstable or uneven. Unstable surfaces bend, shift, or otherwise move when a person puts their weight on them, such as by sitting, leaning, or standing on them. Examples include wobble boards and balance mats. This equipment is meant to prepare people for the different kinds of

HOW RESEARCH EVOLVES

Research in exercise, health, and other branches of science evolves for many reasons. Emerging technology can give researchers new tools for observation and measurement. Small, short studies can lead to larger, longer studies that produce new findings. Belinda Needham, an epidemiology professor, explains, "Many of the things that scientists study are really complicated and hard to observe. . . . We can have greater confidence about a scientific claim if we see that many studies using a variety of techniques reached the same conclusion."[2] Even when there are various studies, Needham emphasizes that scientific understanding can continue to evolve as new technology, approaches, and questions become available.

terrain and conditions they may encounter in everyday life and activities. These may include grass, gravel, snowy and icy ground, mud, cracked sidewalks, and outdoor trails.

Research continues to examine old, current, and emerging trends in stretching and balance and the best ways to implement these exercises. Experts stress the need to continue studying different types of stretching and balance exercises and equipment. They also emphasize the need for ongoing studies among diverse

Balancing on an unstable object can improve core strength.

populations, including athletes, children and teens, young adults, and older adults.

FORMS OF STRETCHING AND BALANCE TODAY

Experts recommend including both dynamic and static stretching and balance exercises in a regular workout routine. Stretching and balance exercises are considered important components of health. These exercises can be stand-alone programs, or they can be integrated

Breathing deeply can help people get the maximum benefit of each stretch.

into aerobic and strength workouts.

Apps, videos, virtual classes, and in-person gyms offer a range of stretching and balance routines. People can find short five-minute exercise videos to follow during breaks throughout the day. Some routines last an hour or more. There are routines that can be done standing, sitting, or supine, which is lying on the back facing upward. There are also routines tailored to different times of day, such as morning stretching and balance routines or stretches around bedtime to relax the body before sleep.

STRETCHING AND BALANCE IN EVERYDAY LIFE

Experts recommend dedicating time several days each week for stretching and balance, but they also advise looking for ways to integrate stretching and balance into everyday activities. For example, there are stretches designed for short work or study breaks that can be done anywhere, even in a library or office chair. People can also do simple balance exercises such as standing on one leg while brushing their teeth, waiting in line, or talking on the phone.

There is also an emphasis on core strength today, especially in balance exercise. Core muscles are located in the hips, pelvis, abdomen, and back. In the context of stretching and balance, core strength focuses on both the large, external muscles and the deep, stabilizing muscles.

New York University's School of Medicine explains that the external core muscles "are more powerful and are typically involved in producing forceful motion."[3] They help the arms and legs move. The deep core muscles "are endurance type muscles that work constantly to stabilize posture," according to health writer Christie Matheson.[4] Side planks are one example of a balance exercise that works the external and deep core muscles.

In addition, stretching and balance exercises today also emphasize mind-body connections to support mental health as well as physical health. Many stretching and balance exercises instruct people to focus on their breathing as they move. Breathing slowly and deliberately helps the body and mind relax.

TRAINING FACILITIES AND GEAR

Regular stretching and balance training is accessible for many people. Anyone with internet access has a wide variety of virtual training options at their fingertips. This is especially true considering that stretching and balance training does not require special gear.

Though no special equipment is required, some people use props to make exercises more comfortable or more challenging. Yoga mats and comfortable, form-fitting clothing are among the more basic items. Plenty of advanced equipment is also available. For example, resistance bands or stretch straps can deepen stretches, and foam blocks can make certain poses easier.

Working with a BOSU ball can build strength through balance.

To make balance work more challenging, exercisers can use equipment that creates an unstable surface. Examples include balance and wobble boards, foam mats, inflatable discs, large exercise balls, BOSU balls, and mini trampolines. People can also use household items in place of stretching and balance equipment. Towels can replace stretching straps. Pillows or cushions can replace foam blocks or serve as unstable surfaces for balance. Walls, counters, and the backs of chairs can offer support in balance exercises.

STRETCHING AND BALANCE AND THE BODY

Experts say stretching and balance exercises improve function in the body's muscles and joints to support day-to-day activities and sports. They may also prevent injuries. The American Academy of Orthopaedic Surgeons explains, "To really reap the benefits of exercise, you need to add flexibility and balance training to the mix."[1]

In addition, experts believe stretching and balance exercises can also improve mental health. The exercises can reduce stress. "With certain stretches, like yoga or Tai Chi, it's getting you in a more relaxed state," says Chris Travers, who studies

Stretching can produce serotonin, which improves mood and reduces stress.

exercise physiology. "It's going to get you to decompress and bring your stress level down and get you in a better frame of mind."[2]

STRETCHING AND THE BODY

Before stretching, muscles may feel sore or tight. There are many reasons a person may have sore or tight muscles. Physical activity is one cause. Hard workouts and intensive activities can cause muscle aches. Long periods of inactivity can also cause soreness. Sitting for long periods can shorten muscles, which makes them feel tight and uncomfortable.

Tight muscles also put the body at risk for muscle and joint injuries. Regular stretching lengthens muscles and helps them stay flexible and elastic. Stretching regularly also improves muscle strength, power, and endurance.

Healthy muscles support healthy joints

THE ROLE OF BREATHING IN STRETCHING

People should pay close attention to their breathing during stretches. Breathing helps release muscle tension and benefits circulation and oxygen levels in the body. Some experts recommend people maintain an abdominal breathing pattern as they stretch. Also known as diaphragmatic or belly breathing, abdominal breathing involves deep inhales that expand the chest and abdomen, followed by long exhales. During exhales, tension in the body decreases, leading to deeper stretches.

The US Centers for Disease Control and Prevention recommends balance exercises twice per week for those ages 65 and older.

by helping them move through full ranges of motion. When joints are exercised, they release synovial fluid, a thick substance that lubricates joints. It also nourishes and protects cartilage, the connective tissue that cushions joints. Joints are healthiest when they regularly move through their full ranges of motion.

Researchers have also found that regular stretching improves blood flow. Blood delivers oxygen and nutrients throughout the body. The brain, muscles, and organs need oxygen and nutrients as fuel. Oxygen and nutrients are also necessary to help the body recover from illness and injury.

In addition, good blood flow aids in removing waste such as carbon dioxide and chemical by-products. These are a natural result of the body's daily functions, including breathing and organ processes. Waste removal is important for healthy body tissue, and regular stretching aids the body in performing these functions.

Stretching also activates the parasympathetic nervous system. This system is responsible for rest and relaxation. It counteracts the sympathetic nervous system, the system responsible for activating the body's stress reaction. Ongoing stress can negatively impact physical and mental health, causing conditions such as muscle and joint pain, high blood pressure, and anxiety. Stretching releases muscle tension and can reduce the level of stress hormones such as cortisol. Researchers also believe that stretching may increase levels of hormones and chemicals responsible for relaxation and positive moods.

STRETCHING PRECAUTIONS

Like many physical activities, stretching can have negative effects on the body when practiced without proper technique or practiced too intensely. To stretch safely, people must be careful to avoid overstretching. Overstretching is when a stretch has gone beyond the body's elastic limit. At that point, the body is at an increased risk of injury. Overstretching can cause strains in tendons or sprains in ligaments.

In order to avoid overstretching, experts advise people to be aware of how their bodies feel during stretches. Stretches should produce a gentle pull in muscles but never pain. People should be patient and allow their bodies to gradually increase in flexibility instead of forcing themselves too far into stretching positions. Experts explain that stretching flexibility increases gradually with regular practice. In addition, people with injuries or chronic health conditions should talk with medical professionals to create the best stretching routines for their needs.

Experts recommend beginning workouts with gentle movement before stretching to decrease the risk of injury.

STRETCHING AND CARDIOVASCULAR HEALTH

Researchers acknowledge that there is still much to learn about how and why stretching changes the body. One topic of ongoing study is the connection between stretching and cardiovascular health. Some research indicates that blood vessels stretch when muscles stretch. The stretch in blood vessels may change their structure, which could decrease blood pressure and stiffness in arteries. High blood pressure and artery stiffness are risk factors for heart attacks and strokes. Regular stretching may mitigate these risks.

A person's flexibility depends on factors such as age, sex, injury history, and the amount of movement they get on a daily basis.

Five to ten minutes of easy walking or biking warms the muscles for static stretching. For dynamic stretching, experts advise beginning with small movements and gradually allowing the movements to become bigger as the muscles warm and loosen.

Another way to decrease risk of injury is to carefully plan the timing and type of stretches when they are used alongside other workouts. Exercise and health-care professionals advise using dynamic stretching before athletic activity and static stretching after athletic activity. Dynamic stretches prepare the body for movement by incorporating motions similar to those required in sports. For example, leg swings mimic the motions performed during running. Dynamic stretching increases muscle temperature and improves the muscles' ability to react. Static stretching after athletic activity and other exercise can help the body cool down and recover.

Props such as bands can aid in dynamic stretching routines.

BALANCE AND THE BODY

Balance is the body's ability to remain stable. Good balance helps people do everyday tasks and exercise with less risk of falling or other injuries. Often, people maintain stability in standing, walking, bending, and other movements without consciously engaging the internal systems that manage balance. Balance exercises can improve the way these systems function, strengthen muscles, keep joints healthy, and promote good posture.

Balance requires people to keep their center of gravity over a base of support. The center of gravity is the midpoint of the body's weight. If a person is standing, the center of gravity is usually around the belly button. The base of support refers to the body parts in contact with the ground or the supporting surface. Feet are usually the base of support. The base of support can change and grow larger and smaller throughout everyday movements such as walking, kneeling, bending, leaning, and other activities. These activities also shift the body's weight and center of gravity, which challenges balance.

Various systems in the body maintain balance. These include the sensory, musculoskeletal, and nervous systems. Together, these systems gather information, interpret information, and move the body.

The visual and vestibular systems are two sensory systems important to balance. The visual system is the

Even an activity as simple as walking has a balance component.

pathway from the eyes to the brain. Cleveland Clinic explains, "Your eyes send impulses to your brain that show where your body is in relation to other objects."[3]

People experiencing frequent dizziness and balance issues may have vestibular issues.

The vestibular system is located in the inner ear. It includes three semicircular canals and two organs, called the utricle and the saccule. The vestibular system senses when the head moves up and down, tilts, or turns. Cells alert the brain to this movement through nerves.

Muscles also have sensory receptors. They send information to the brain, alerting it when muscles lengthen and shorten and communicating how quickly the changes occur. Muscle sensory receptors contribute to the body's awareness of its position and movements, a concept known as proprioception.

The nervous system is also integral to balance. The nervous system includes the brain, spinal cord, and nerves. It controls voluntary, or conscious, movement and involuntary reactions in the body. Muscles and the nerves that send messages between the brain and muscles make up the neuromuscular system.

Through these systems, the brain and muscles create movement and control posture, which supports balance. The National Cancer Institute explains, "Posture, such as sitting and standing, is maintained as a result of muscle contraction. The skeletal muscles are

PROGRESSIVE MUSCLE RELAXATION

Progressive muscle relaxation (PMR) is an exercise that involves tensing and relaxing muscle groups. It trains the body and brain to tell the difference between feeling tense and feeling relaxed. PMR can improve body awareness and relieve stress. To practice PMR, get in a comfortable position. Relax your body. Then, tense one part of your body. For example, start by tensing the toes. After five seconds, release the tension. Rest 15 to 30 seconds. Repeat with the feet. Move up through the body, tensing each muscle group. When finished, the body should feel loose and relaxed.

continually making fine adjustments that hold the body in stationary positions."[4]

The nervous system directs these adjustments even when people are not aware of them. Most often when people lose their balance, it is because there is a disruption in communication among the sensory, muscular, and nervous systems. Research studies show that balance training can improve communication among these systems.

Balance exercises engage sensory and neuromuscular systems, enhancing the brain's ability to process the information it receives from these systems. This in turn improves the brain and body's ability to interact to maintain balance.

When standing on an unstable surface, the body's core works to maintain balance.

CHAPTER FOUR

STATIC STRETCHING

Experts recommend performing static stretching routines for at least ten minutes a day two to three days each week. Regular static stretching should target all major muscle groups. Routines should vary throughout the week, with some focusing on the upper body and some focusing on the lower body.

Static stretching can be used as a cooldown after sports activities, aerobic exercise, or strength training. It can also be done as its own workout. If static stretching is being done as a separate routine, experts advise starting with five to ten minutes of light activity such as walking or dynamic stretching to warm up the body. These activities make the transition to static stretching much safer.

Consistent static stretching helps increase range of motion.

GUIDELINES FOR STATIC STRETCHING

Guidelines vary as to the proper length of time to hold each static stretch. Medical professional Mary Gavin recommends 10 to 30 seconds per stretch, which can be done one to four times.[1] If repeating a stretch, rest between each set to avoid overstretching. If a stretch targets one side of the body at a time, make sure to repeat the stretch on the opposite side.

Experts also offer advice on stretching safely. A stretching guide from the University of Georgia explains, "It is better to understretch than to overstretch." To avoid overstretching, the guide explains, "Always be at a point where you can stretch further, and never at a point where you have gone as far as you can go."[2] In addition, move slowly into static stretches, and do not use bouncing or force to deepen stretches.

Experts also caution people to protect their joints during stretches. The easiest way is to make sure joints such as knees and elbows are not locked when stretching. The International Sports Sciences Association explains that locking means pressing the joint "back as far as possible so that there is no bend."[3] Locking can stress the joint and stretch the ligaments, tendons, and cartilage too far. Slight bends in the knees and elbows protect those joints.

Good posture is another way to protect yourself during stretches. When stretching, your shoulders and

Overstretching can cause issues such as soreness, bruising, and muscle spasms.

hips should be level. Unless otherwise mentioned, your chin should be parallel to the ground, and your back should have a neutral position, meaning the spine does not slump forward or arch back.

STATIC STRETCHES FOR THE UPPER BODY

Static stretching for the upper body targets muscles and joints in the neck, upper back, shoulders, chest, arms, and wrists. Many upper body stretches target more than one muscle at a time. It is common for upper body muscles to grow tight from stress and daily activities. In fact, tension in the neck and upper body is so common

Stretches can be done several times per day if needed.

that the area is nicknamed the Tension Triangle. Static stretching releases this tension and also improves overall body health.

It is important to rest before repeating a stretch to avoid overstretching. If you notice any pain, tingling, or numbness after you exercise, check with a doctor before returning to stretching, as this may be a sign of injury.

Upper back stretches release tension in the upper back and neck. One stretch can be done from a sitting or standing position. To perform the stretch, lace your fingers together and reach your arms straight ahead, parallel to the floor. Round your back, and dip your chin toward your chest, until your ears are between your arms. Pull your belly button toward your back to deepen the stretch. Hold the stretch for 10 to 15 seconds.[4]

A pectoral stretch typically uses an opposing motion to upper back stretches. These stretches open the chest. The pectoral muscles connect the upper arm and shoulder bones to the front of the chest. They assist with movement in the shoulders and arms. One way to do a pectoral stretch is to stand in the middle of an open doorway. Bend your elbows to a 90-degree angle, and place one forearm on each side of the doorway. Your elbows should be level with your shoulders, which should be relaxed but not shrugged.

TECH NECK

Tech Neck is the nickname given to neck pain that comes from bending over electronic devices. An article from the University of Texas Southwestern Medical Center explains, "The typical adult head weighs 10–12 pounds [4.5–5.4 kg], but bending it forward at a 45-degree angle—not unusual when looking at a cellphone—increases the amount of force on the neck to nearly 50 pounds [23 kg]."[5] When done repeatedly, this increased force can cause neck pain or injury. Experts recommend people keep devices at eye level to reduce neck strain. Regular stretching and exercise can also help mitigate and prevent neck pain.

If your body feels too tight with your elbows at shoulder level, lower them a little bit. Take a small, careful step forward with one foot, keeping your spine tall. Step forward just enough to feel a stretch across your chest and the front of your shoulders.

Some stretches work the arms along with the shoulders and chest. One such stretch involves bringing the arms behind the head and back. Use a towel or an exercise band to assist with this stretch.

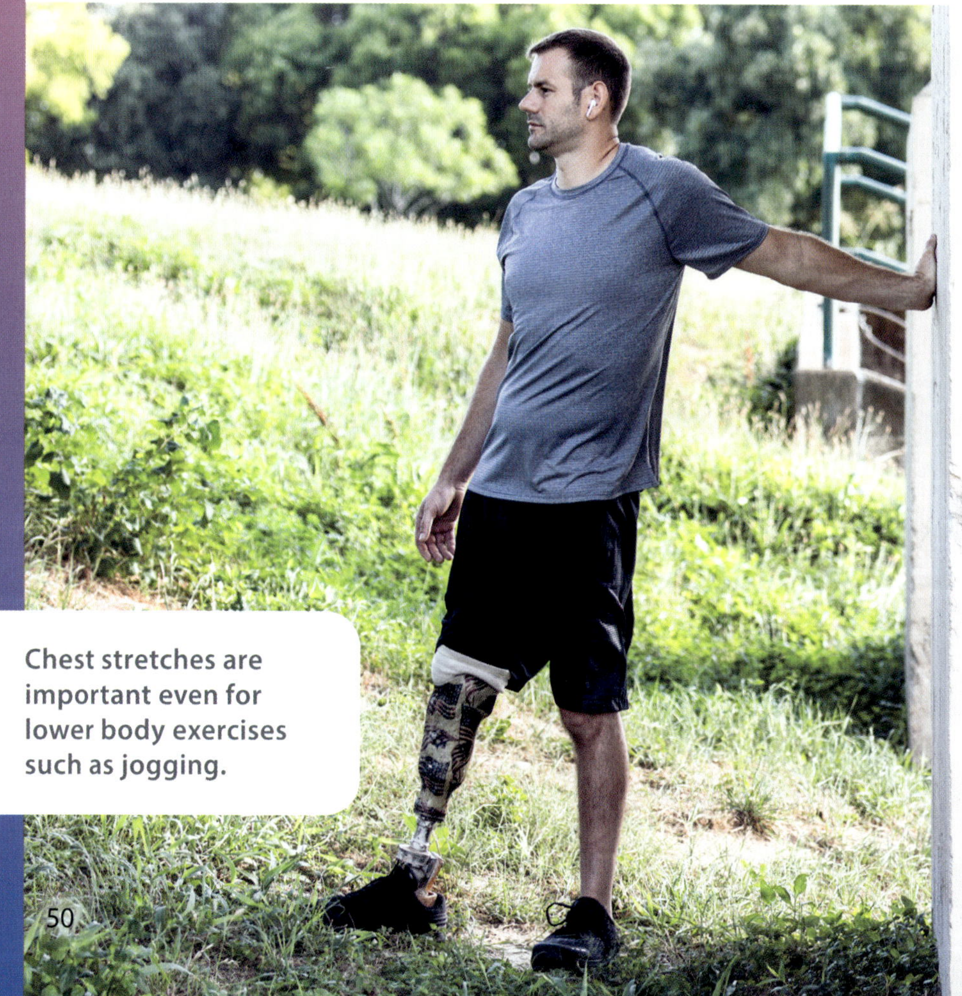

Chest stretches are important even for lower body exercises such as jogging.

Grasp one end of the towel in one hand, and raise your arm over your head. Let your other hand hang by your side for now. Bend your raised arm's elbow so your hand reaches for your upper back and the towel hangs behind your back. Reach the other arm behind your back to grasp the towel.

Gently pull the top hand upward and the bottom hand downward. Keep your raised elbow open and pointing mostly upward. The stretch should create an open feeling through your chest and shoulders. It should also stretch your triceps, the muscles in the back of the arm between the elbow and shoulder.

The biceps sit between the elbows and shoulders on the front of the arm. They act as opposing muscles to the triceps. To stretch the biceps, sit or stand with your back straight and your arms raised out to your sides at shoulder height. With your palms facing forward, make fists, point your thumbs upward, and hold the stretch. Then turn your thumbs to point down so your palms face backward. Hold each position for your desired length of time.

Forearm and wrist stretches can also be done from a sitting or standing position. They keep the forearms and wrists healthy for everyday activities such as typing or writing. These stretches are also used by golfers, tennis players, and other athletes who require flexible wrists. One forearm and wrist stretch involves rotating your wrists.

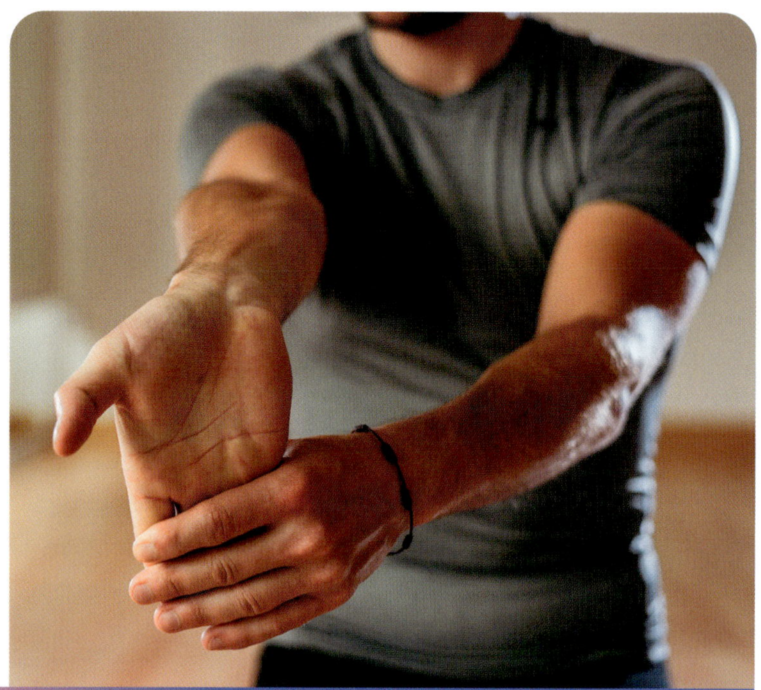

This position stretches the biceps and forearm muscles and also helps with wrist mobility.

To begin, raise one arm straight in front of your body, parallel to the ground with your palm facing up. Use your other hand to pull your fingers on your stretching hand gently downward and back toward your body. There should be a slight stretch through the underside of your wrist and forearm.

After holding the stretch, release and turn your palm down toward the ground. Gently pull your fingers down and toward your body. You should feel a light stretch along the top of your wrist and forearm. Repeat with the other hand.

STATIC STRETCHES FOR THE TORSO

Static stretches for the torso target the core muscles. Often, these stretches work more than one core muscle at a time. For example, the side bend stretch works the latissimus dorsi muscle in the mid and low back as well as the oblique muscles on the sides of the body. It also works the intercostal muscles, the muscles between the ribs.

From a standing position, lift your left arm straight up over your shoulder with your palm facing toward your body. Keep your right arm loose. Gently lean toward your right side, and make sure your hips and shoulders stay facing forward. Let your neck relax as you

One variation of a side bend is often called the teapot stretch because of the shape the body makes.

look down toward your right hand. After holding for your desired length of time, repeat with the opposite arm.

Spinal twists are another stretch that targets many parts of the torso. Regularly performing twists builds mobility and flexibility in the spine. The seated spinal twist is a simple stretch done on the floor.

Sit with your legs straight in front of your body. Bend your left knee and cross it over your opposite leg. Plant your foot outside your right thigh. Place your left hand on the ground behind you for support. Gently press your right arm against your left leg and twist your upper body to the left. The stretch from the twist should extend to your abdominal, back, shoulder, and neck muscles, as well as your hips and gluteus muscles, or glutes. Switch legs and twist in the other direction.

Prop-ups are another common stretch for the torso. This stretch is similar to the sphinx pose

BACK CRACKING

Some people occasionally hear a cracking sound when they do back stretches. Medical professionals say this cracking sound is normal as long as it is not painful. The noise is caused by gas bubbles popping within the spine's synovial fluid. The fluid lubricates the back's facet joints, which are the joints that connect the vertebra bones in the spine. Gas bubbles form and pop in the synovial fluid as the back goes through various movements during daily activities, exercise, and stretching. However, if back cracking causes pain, experts advise seeing a doctor.

FITNESS SNAPSHOT

SEATED SPINAL TWIST

Twist body toward arm, keeping spine tall

Place arm outside knee and press against leg

Plant one foot behind opposite knee

Use second arm for support

Leave bottom leg straight

THE WORLD'S GREATEST STRETCH

The World's Greatest Stretch earned its name due to the many parts of the body it benefits. The stretch targets the shoulders, spine, hips, glutes, hamstrings, and quadriceps. Begin in a plank position with your palms flat on the ground. Then, bring your left foot forward and place it on the ground by your left hand. Lift your left hand off the floor, bending the elbow in a 90-degree angle. Reach your left elbow down toward your right hand. Finally, lift your left arm up toward the ceiling, twisting the body to open the chest. Repeat on the other side.

in yoga and stretches the chest, abdominal, and back muscles. Start by lying face down on the floor. Prop yourself up on your elbows to lift your chest and head off the floor.

Make sure your chest stays open and your head and neck are neutral. Keep your elbows directly under your shoulders and your forearms facing straight forward on the floor. Let your lower body lie flat against the ground, and focus on lengthening the spine.

The knees-to-chest stretch is a lower back stretch done on the floor. Lie down on your back, then bend your knees and bring them to your chest. Rest your hands below your knees or behind your thighs, and use them to gently draw your knees closer to your chest. Keep your lower back on the floor throughout. To try a variation of this stretch, lie supine and bring only one leg to your chest, leaving the other flat on the ground.

STATIC STRETCHES FOR THE LOWER BODY

The major muscle groups in the lower body are the hamstrings, quadriceps, calves, and glutes. Each of these groups has more than one muscle. The hamstrings and quadriceps each have four muscles, the glutes have three, and the calves have two. In addition, the hips have flexor, abductor, and adductor muscles. Lower body muscles can grow tight from repetitive use in sports and from everyday activities such as sitting.

The hamstring and calf muscles are both in the back of the legs. The calf muscles lie in the lower part of the leg, while the hamstrings are in the upper leg. A standing stretch can target both of these muscle groups at the same time.

Start by standing up straight. Place one foot slightly in front of you with just the heel touching the ground. Bend your back knee and lean forward by pushing your hips back. Keep your back straight and your shoulders relaxed. Pull the toes of your front foot back toward the shin and continue moving your hips back and down until you feel a mild stretch in your calf and hamstring muscles. Do not push back forcefully through your front knee. Repeat on the other leg.

The quadriceps are in the front of the upper leg. Stretching the quadriceps while standing requires some balance. Stand near a wall, chair back, counter, or other sturdy object for help with balance if needed. Lift your left foot off the ground and bend the leg behind your body. Reach back with your left hand and take hold of your ankle or the top of your foot. If you can't reach your ankle, loop a towel or stretching strap around your foot and grab onto that instead.

Gently pull your ankle toward your glutes to create a stretch in the front of your leg. Engage your core and make sure your hips are neutral so you stand tall and your back doesn't arch. Keep your knees close together and the hips level and facing forward. Repeat with your other leg.

The figure four stretch targets muscles in the hips and glutes. Some people call this stretch a floor pretzel because of the shape the legs make. Lie on your back with your knees bent and feet on the floor. Move your right leg to place your right ankle on your left thigh just above the knee. Your right shin should be parallel to the floor. Your right knee should point outward to the side, creating a triangular shape like the number four.

Flex your right foot so the toes reach toward the right knee. Reach between your legs and clasp your hands behind your left thigh. Keep your right knee pointing outward throughout. Lift your left foot off the floor and gently pull your legs toward your chest to create a stretch in your hip and glutes of the right leg. After holding for your desired length of time, repeat the stretch with your opposite leg.

The quadriceps stretch is very useful both before and after running.

CHAPTER

DYNAMIC STRETCHING

Dynamic stretching is stretching through movement. This movement warms the muscles and guides the joints through their range of motion. Athletes use dynamic stretching as part of their warm-ups because it prepares the body for more intense activity. Dynamic stretching can also be used as a warm-up before static stretching or as an independent workout to loosen the body.

Dynamic stretching movements should be continuous, smooth, and controlled. Dynamic stretching is described as "rhythmic movements" by Children's Mercy Hospital in Kansas City, Missouri.[1] They begin small and can gradually grow larger as the body loosens throughout the repetitions. The movements should not be forced or jerky.

Dynamic stretching is good preparation for athletic activities.

To keep the body stable during dynamic stretches, engage the core muscles. Engaging the core means gently contracting the stomach muscles. Contracting the core muscles feels like pulling them gently inward. To perform safe and effective dynamic stretching, maintain good posture and make sure to keep the joints unlocked.

The number of repetitions for dynamic stretches varies based on individual needs. The Cleveland Clinic recommends performing each dynamic stretch ten to 20 times.[2] For stretches that work one side of the body at a time, people should perform the same number of stretches on each side.

DYNAMIC STRETCHES FOR THE NECK AND UPPER BODY

Dynamic neck stretches can be performed anywhere. To do a dynamic neck stretch, sit or stand with your upper body relaxed and your eyes looking forward. Keep your head level and slowly rotate your neck to look left and right. Pause for two to three seconds on each side. Once your neck has been stretched to each side, shift the movement so that you are alternating up and down. Slowly tilt your chin upward, then slowly tilt it downward. This is also called the yes stretch, as it looks like a slow version of nodding.

Neck rotations can create a greater range of motion.

Arm circles are dynamic stretches that improve mobility in the shoulders. This stretch is also good for the biceps and triceps. Begin by standing with your feet shoulder-distance apart. Raise your arms out to the sides so they are parallel to the ground. Make small circles with your arms. The circles can get bigger as your body loosens

FITNESS SNAPSHOT

ARM CIRCLES

Keep arms parallel to the ground

Palms face forward

Rotate arms forward

Do same number of reps rotating the other way

Stand with feet shoulder-width apart

through the stretch. After ten to 20 circles, repeat the arm circles in the opposite direction.

Arm swings are another dynamic shoulder stretch. This exercise stretches the chest and back and lengthens the muscles in the torso. To perform the stretch, stand with your feet shoulder-width apart and arms straight out from your sides. Bring your arms up and swing them in front of your chest, crossing one arm over the other. Stop the motion when you feel your arms are fully stretched. Swing your arms out and backward, reaching just behind you to open up your chest. Repeat this motion ten to 20 times, alternating your top and bottom arms with each swing.

Arm swings can also move up and down. Begin by raising both arms directly above your shoulders with palms facing each other. Then, keeping your arms straight, swing your arms down until they are

DYNAMIC WRIST AND ANKLE STRETCHES

Wrist and ankle circles are dynamic stretches that improve range of motion and release tightness in the muscles and tendons of the wrists and ankles. To perform wrist circles, make loose fists and roll the wrists ten times in one direction. Repeat the motion ten times in the other direction. Ankle circles, also known as ankle rolls, are performed similarly. Start by lifting one foot off the ground. Gently roll the ankle of the raised foot as if drawing a circle with the toes. Do ten circles in one direction then another ten in the opposite direction. Repeat with the other ankle.

beside your hips. Swing your arms back up to starting position, making sure not to arch the lower back too much. Perform these swings with both arms at once, or do one side at a time.

DYNAMIC STRETCHES FOR THE TORSO

Dynamic torso stretches work the core muscles of the back, stomach, and hips. They often involve gentle twisting and bending motions. These stretches move the torso forward and backward, side to side, and through rotations. Torso twists build mobility and flexibility in the spine.

The body performs these kinds of lifting and twisting movements every day. This type of movement is important in sports that involve throwing. It is also helpful for athletes who swing bats or rackets.

A basic standing torso twist, also known as a trunk rotation, is one kind of dynamic torso stretch. Start by standing with your feet shoulder-width apart and your body relaxed. Bend your elbows at a 90-degree angle and hold them tight to the sides of your body. Gently twist from side to side, taking care not to overstretch.

Dynamic side bends curve and stretch the oblique and intercostal muscles on the sides of the body. This stretch also helps to release tension in the back muscles near the spine. To perform the dynamic side bend stretch, stand with your feet shoulder-width apart and your body relaxed. Keep your arms loose by your sides. Slowly and smoothly, lean to one side, then to the other side. Make sure your shoulders and hips stay facing forward. The motion should be gentle and rocking. Breathe out as you bend to each side, and inhale as you return to the vertical position.

For a dynamic stretch that moves the spine forward and back, perform an exaggerated slouch and straightening motion. Begin by sitting in a chair in a

The torso twist stretch mimics the movement of a golf swing.

FITNESS SNAPSHOT
DYNAMIC SIDE BENDS
Lean hips to one side and stretch arm up and away from hips
Head, chest, and hips face forward
Keep arm by side
Stand with feet shoulder-width apart

slouched position. Round your shoulders forward and let your head hang down. Then, pull your shoulders back and straighten your head to sit up tall. Arch your lower back slightly to create a small exaggeration in the natural curve of your spine. Move between slouching and arching, pausing for roughly two to three seconds in each position.

The seated windshield wiper stretch targets the hips and core. Begin seated on the floor with your knees bent. The soles of your feet should be flat on the ground and a little more than hip-width apart. Lay your palms on the ground behind your body with your fingers turned away from you. Lean back slightly to stretch your shoulders.

While leaning back, lower your knees gently to one side. Your knees should be next to each other rather than stacked. After a short pause, raise your knees back to their starting position, then lower them to the other side. This motion should stretch your lower back and hips.

FOAM ROLLING

Foam rolling helps massage and place pressure on muscles. Athletes lower their bodies onto the rollers and press the sore muscles against the foam. They can roll back and forth to increase the pressure. Foam rolling has been practiced since the 1980s and has become increasingly popular in exercise warm-ups and cooldowns. Studies indicate foam rolling can decrease tension in the body, relieve muscle soreness, and improve range of motion.

Bands can be used to provide added resistance to leg swings.

DYNAMIC STRETCHES FOR THE LOWER BODY

Similar to upper-body dynamic stretches, lower-body dynamic stretches often use controlled movements. Leg swings target many parts of the lower body, including the hips, glutes, groin, quadriceps, hamstrings, and calves. These movements are also beneficial for the feet and ankles. Leg swings require some balance, so stand near a wall, chair, or other supportive surface. Hold on to the surface as needed through the movements.

There are two primary forms of leg swings. The first is the forward-backward leg swing. Begin by standing on one leg with a slight bend at the knee. Lift your other leg off the ground. While keeping your lifted leg as straight as possible, swing the leg first in front, then behind your body. Engage your core muscles to maintain balance and straight posture. As the motions continue, your leg muscles may start to feel looser, and the swings may get bigger. Repeat with the other leg.

The second form of leg swings is the side-to-side swing. As with the forward swing, stand on one leg with a slight bend in your knee, then lift your other leg off the ground. Keeping your lifted leg as straight as possible, raise it out to the side away from your body. Swing to cross it in front of your body and then out to the side again. Keep the front of your body square and do not twist into the swings through your torso. Repeat the swings on your opposite leg.

Knee lift stretches target the glutes. Stand with your feet shoulder-width apart. Lift one leg and bend your knee to bring it up toward your chest. Be careful to keep your hips level.

TRAVELING DYNAMIC STRETCHES

Adding walking is a good way to bring additional movement to lower body dynamic stretches. Examples include knee lift stretches and dynamic quadriceps stretches. To add walking to these stretches, place the lifted leg one step forward when lowering it from the stretch. Incorporating walking in dynamic stretches can be especially helpful when using these exercises as part of a warm-up for other activities.

To deepen the stretch, clasp your hands around your lifted knee and gently pull it upward and toward your body. Hold the clasp for one second, release and lower your leg. Repeat this motion with your other leg.

Dynamic quadricep stretches are a reverse motion to knee lifts. Stand with your feet hip-width apart. Bend one leg back to lift that heel toward your glutes. Keep your hips level and facing forward through the motion. There should be a stretch in the thigh area at the front of your raised leg. Bring your foot to the ground before repeating the motion with your other leg.

Hamstring scoops target the hamstrings and calves. Start by standing up straight. Place one foot in front of

Knee lifts can benefit the glutes, thighs, calves, and ankles.

Loosening up the ankles before exercise can release tension in the calves.

you with just the heel touching the ground. Slightly bend the knee of your back leg and push your hips back to lean forward. Make sure to keep your back straight, shoulders relaxed, and your arms hanging at your sides. Pull the toes of your front foot back toward your shin until there is a mild stretch in your calf and hamstring muscles.

In one fluid motion, hinge forward even deeper at the hips, keeping your front leg straight but not locked at the knee. Reach toward your feet with your arms straight, and move them up in a scooping motion. Straighten back up, ending with your arms raised above your shoulders. Alternate legs, or repeat on the same side before working the other leg.

STATIC BALANCE

Static balance is how the body remains stable and steady in still positions such as sitting and standing. It may seem maintaining stillness would be an easy thing for most people. However, even in still positions, the body works subconsciously against internal movements called internal perturbations.

To highlight the role of balance in standing, stand upright and close your eyes. You will feel the gentle movements in your body. These movements result in what is called postural sway, which is the ongoing adjustments muscles make to keep the body upright and centered. These adjustments occur in the ankles and legs. Core muscles are also important in balance and stability. The nervous system regulates these adjustments,

Many yoga poses incorporate static balance.

and balance training improves the body's ability to make these changes.

GUIDELINES FOR STATIC BALANCE EXERCISE

Possessing strong balance provides the foundation for all forms of exercise. "If you're a beginning exerciser, balance and stability may be a challenge," says certified personal trainer Paige Waehner, "which is a great reason to focus on these areas of fitness before moving on to more challenging workouts."[1] Even small amounts of regular training can benefit balance ability. This training can be incorporated into other exercise routines or into daily life.

When first starting to improve balance, begin with simple exercises before progressing to more challenging ones. Experts advise beginners to first practice on a firm, even floor.

BALANCE GAMES

Many activities that young children participate in are also developing important concepts of stability and balance that will carry into later life. Even something as simple as riding a swing develops a young person's core and trunk muscles. When the swing moves in an unpredictable way, the child's muscles must work harder to compensate. Hopscotch is another simple game that teaches young children complicated methods of balance as they maneuver on one leg. "Hopscotch is ingeniously designed to challenge children's sense of balance and orientation," say child development expert Gill Connell and coauthor Cheryl McCarthy.[2]

Consider standing near a sturdy surface to touch or hold on to as needed when trying new exercises. Support surfaces can include a wall, counter, or the back of a chair. Engaging the core muscles by gently contracting them also helps with stability in balance exercises.

STATIC TWO-LEG BALANCE EXERCISES

Balance exercises for beginners involve standing straight and still on both feet. The exercises become more challenging with varied foot placements and holding for more time. The goal in each variation is to hold the position with proper form for ten seconds and progress toward holding the position for 60 seconds.

You should hold a position only for as long as you can maintain proper form and keep equal body weight on each foot. You should also maintain level hips, a neutral spine position, and relaxed, level shoulders. As your skill grows, you can try performing multiple sets of each exercise.

A good exercise to begin with is standing with your feet together so they touch. Your feet should be side by side, toes facing forward. This position narrows your base of support, making it harder to balance than if your feet are shoulder-width apart.

This feet-together standing exercise can also increase your awareness of the mechanics of balance. You may feel muscles in your legs and core acting to reduce postural sway and hold your body in position. Learning to engage these muscles consciously is important for maintaining stability after moving on to more challenging balance exercises.

Instead of standing with your feet side by side, you can place one foot in front of the other in a tandem stance. The heel of your front foot should touch the toes of your back foot. This position creates an even narrower base of support than standing with your feet together. If the tandem stance is too difficult, use a semi-tandem stance first and work up to tandem. In this type of stance, your feet are staggered slightly, with the toes of your back foot touching the inside arch of your front foot.

SINGLE-LEG BALANCE EXERCISES

Single-leg balance exercises are more difficult than double-leg exercises. In these exercises, one leg supports your full body weight. This leg is known as the stance leg.

Similar to double-leg exercises, there are variations for single-leg balance work. A basic single-leg balance exercise involves standing on one leg while the other is bent at the knee in front of or behind your body. You can also try straightening your lifted leg and holding your foot either in front of your body or to the side.

For all single-leg balance exercises, it is important to keep a slight bend in your stance leg. Doing so will protect the knee joint. Your hips should be level. Placing your hands on your hips is a good way to check whether they are even.

Another way to keep your hips level is to focus on engaging your leg muscles and squeezing your glutes.

There are many variations to static balance stances. Each can be customized to the exerciser's ability level.

FITNESS SNAPSHOT

SINGLE-LEG STATIC BALANCE

Use core to stay upright and tall

Hold for desired amount of time

Variation: Straighten lifted leg or hold behind standing leg

Stand on one leg without locking knee

Bend lifted leg at knee

Distribute weight evenly through foot

One balance exercise uses the movements of a Romanian dead lift, a common weight-lifting exercise.

Imagine your stance leg pushing against the ground to keep your body lifted. Avoid curling your toes to grip onto the floor for balance. Perform single-leg balance exercises for the same amount of time on each side to ensure even training.

A more challenging version of the single-leg balance exercise involves raising one leg behind your body. Lower your chest to be parallel to the ground and raise your leg to waist level. Hold your arms out to the sides in a T or reach them in front of your body in line with your shoulders.

INCREASING THE DIFFICULTY IN STANDING STATIC BALANCE

There are several techniques to make standing balance exercises more challenging. One such technique is to close your eyes. Closing the eyes removes input from your body's visual balance system. One research study tested adults in many age groups and found the average single-leg balance time to be about 33 seconds. That time decreased to eight seconds when the subject's eyes were closed.[3]

Changing the position of your head is another technique to make standing balance more difficult. While standing in a static balance exercise, turn your head left, right, up, and down. Closing your eyes while turning your head makes balance even more

REACTIVE BALANCE

Reactive balance is the body's ability to regain balance and avoid falling during unexpected disruptions, also known as external perturbations. These disruptions occur every day. They may be caused by tripping over a crack in a sidewalk or by being jostled while standing in a bus. Balance training with challenges such as closing your eyes or exercising on an unstable surface can help to improve reactive balance.

difficult. Begin head turns slowly and maintain control to avoid straining your neck.

Static balance exercises also become more difficult when performed on unstable surfaces. Surfaces such as balance mats, wobble boards, or BOSU balls exaggerate the effects of postural sway. If you don't have these items, you can place a pillow or cushion on the floor to stand on as an unstable surface.

Using weights is yet another way to progress a static standing balance move. According to the Mayo Clinic, adding weights to balance exercises also activates the core muscles. When one part of the body lifts a weighted object, muscles in other parts of the body, especially the core, contract to provide stability. People can use free weights, medicine balls, or even household objects such as water bottles or cans of food as weights.

To incorporate weight exercises and core

THE CORE CHALLENGE OF KNEELING

Performing weight-training exercises while kneeling can challenge both balance and the core. On the website Stack, a strength and conditioning specialist wrote that "core muscles are forced to work harder while kneeling" than while standing.[4] Weight lifting while half kneeling is also a good way to train the core and test balance. Half kneeling means kneeling on one leg. The other knee is bent to a 90-degree angle in front of your body with your foot flat on the ground.

Physiotherapy often includes static balance moves to aid injury recovery.

strength into static balance, try holding a single-leg stance while doing biceps curls or an overhead press. Tighten your core and glutes to help with balance and stability. Maintain a neutral spine throughout the exercises.

Another advancement for single-leg balance is to pass a weight from one side of the body to the other. For one method, hold a weight in one hand down at your hip. Slowly raise your arm out to the side and overhead. When your arm extends over your shoulder, carefully pass the weight to your other hand and lower that arm down to your hip. It may help to hold your lifted leg straight and in front of your body.

BALANCE BOARD TECHNOLOGY

Modern balance boards were invented in the 1950s. One design, called the Bongo Board, came from Stanley Washburn Jr., an American pilot in World War II (1939–1945). The board is a piece of wood laid over a circular roller.

Washburn said he came up with the idea after observing children on the coast of western Africa balancing on a flat piece of wood placed atop a log. Washburn was intrigued and constructed his first Bongo Board as a Christmas present for his daughter. The boards sold successfully as children's toys, and eventually athletes began to use them to practice balance.

Today, companies have created many different types of balance boards in many shapes and sizes. There are balance boards designed for training in sports such as soccer, surfing, and skateboarding. There are also balance boards designed to be used with standing desks. Some companies have

Stanley Washburn gave the first Bongo Board to his daughter in 1952.

made balance boards for video games. Others have developed balance boards to use with virtual reality games and apps.

Despite the boards' popularity, experts emphasize that they are not the only way to practice balance. They are also not necessarily the best way to train for sports. As skateboarders Per Welinder and Peter Whitley wrote in their book *Mastering Skateboarding*, "You will find myriad balancing toys, mock skateboards, and devices that promise to improve your skating. The best way to improve your skateboarding balance is simply by riding a skateboard."[5]

DYNAMIC BALANCE

Dynamic balance incorporates a variety of movements. Some of these are functional, which means they prepare the body for movements performed in everyday life. Others are more challenging movements that improve athletic ability. In both cases, dynamic balance both relies on and helps build core strength.

Experts recommend similar safety guidelines to those used in static balance. Begin with simple exercises. Progress to harder exercises as balance ability improves. Perform the exercises near a sturdy object or surface to hold on to if needed. For effective and safe motion in dynamic balance training, Shriya Maharaj, a certified exercise physiologist, explains, "Keep your posture tall and focus on quality of movement rather than speed."[1]

Without a stable sense of dynamic balance, simply walking would be a challenge.

FROM STATIC TO DYNAMIC

Basic dynamic balance exercises build on static balance exercises by adding movement. One is tandem walking. As with the static tandem stance, place one foot directly in front of the other so the heel of your front foot touches the toes of your back foot. Move forward in a straight line, placing one foot in front of the other, like walking on a balance beam or tightrope. Aim for at least 15 steps in a row.

Return to the starting position by tandem walking backward, moving your front foot so that your toes touch the heel of your back foot. Tandem walking backward should be more challenging than walking forward. Try to do three to four sets of forward and backward tandem walking.

Grapevines are another walking exercise, which involves repeatedly crossing one foot over the other to walk sideways. To start the exercise, begin with your feet together. Step your left foot over

THE FARMER'S WALK

The farmer's walk is a simple exercise to improve dynamic balance and whole-body strength. The exercise gets its name because the movement resembles a farmer carrying heavy equipment in each hand. To perform the farmer's walk, let your arms hang by your sides with a weight in each hand. Walk straight forward. Begin with a distance of ten yards (9 m). You can change the difficulty by varying the weight or the distance.

the other, crossing your left leg in front of your body and landing just on the outside of your right foot. Uncross your feet by moving your right foot beside your left foot. Take another step, repeating the crossing motion, but cross your left leg behind your body rather than in front of it. Continue the steps, alternating front and back crosses. As you move, keep your body square and facing forward. After completing about ten steps in one direction, repeat in the opposite direction. Try to do three sets.

Adding leg movements to single-leg standing is another way to transform static balance exercises into

Tightrope walking is an extreme example of dynamic balance.

FITNESS SNAPSHOT

GRAPEVINES

dynamic balance exercises. The ice skaters exercise is one example. Stand on one foot, lifting the other leg in front of the body. Bend your lifted leg 90 degrees.

Swing your lifted leg to the side and then behind your body to make a half-circle motion. The motion should be slow and fluid. Without stopping, reverse and swing your leg forward. Perform the exercise ten times before repeating with the opposite leg. You can increase the difficulty of the exercise by lifting your leg higher.

ADDING REACHES TO CHALLENGE BALANCE

Reaching during balance exercises is one way to increase an exercise's difficulty. Reaching also builds core strength. A standing march is a balance exercise that can incorporate reaching. To begin the exercise, stand with your feet hip-width apart. Lift one arm straight up over your shoulder. Simultaneously lift your opposite leg to about hip height, keeping the knee bent at 90 degrees. Lower both limbs and repeat with the opposite arm and leg, still standing in place.

Engage your core throughout the movement. As you march, your hips and shoulders should remain level, even as your arms and legs move up and down. Aim for three sets of 12 to 15 repetitions.

To make standing marches more difficult, add a weight in one hand. As you march, lift the weight straight up, and hold it steady over your shoulder. Keep the weight lifted as you march in place for 30 to 45 seconds. Move the weight to your opposite hand and march again for the same length of time. Holding weight on just one side of the body challenges your core muscles because they must work to stabilize the imbalance.

Multidirectional reaches are another balance exercise that includes movement in the upper and lower body. One involves a variation of the single-leg Romanian dead lift. Stand on one leg with a slight bend in your knee and your other leg lifted slightly behind you. Imagine three dots placed in a triangle formation in front of your stance leg, one to the left, one in front of the leg, and one to the right. It can be helpful to place cones or other objects where the dots would be.

Keep a straight back, hinge forward at the hips, move one arm down, and extend toward to the first dot. Both legs stay straight, and try to raise your lifted leg higher off the ground if you're able. Ensure that your shoulders and hips remain square to the middle dot; the movement should not come from twisting your body open. As you reach toward the dot, keep your chest parallel to the floor and your core muscles engaged. Then, engage your glutes in order to rise to a standing position. After completing the three reaches on one leg, switch to the other leg. Try to perform two to three sets of ten to 12 repetitions.

FITNESS SNAPSHOT

STANDING MARCH

BALANCE IN COMMON STRENGTH EXERCISES

Many exercises used in strength training also serve as balance exercises. Examples include calf raises, squats, and lunges. They shift the body's base of support and center of gravity, which challenges balance. Calf raises, for example, shift the body's support from the whole foot to only the ball of the foot. In addition, calf raises also target important balance muscles in the ankles, feet, and calves. Plyometric exercises such as hopping, jumping, and bounding also involve balance.

Multidirectional reaches might seem like a technical balance exercise, but they are similar to movements in daily life. You use this kind of motion when you lean down to pick something up. You can even practice this type of exercise within your day-to-day activities. Chris Freytag, a certified personal trainer and fitness instructor, suggests, "If you drop your keys or wallet, reach over to pick them up on one leg with the other leg lifting straight into the air behind you and engage your abs."[2]

FLOOR EXERCISES FOR DYNAMIC BALANCE AND CORE STRENGTH

Working on the ground from seated or supine positions provides additional ways to challenge balance. These dynamic movements can also improve core strength. Some people prefer to use an exercise mat during this type of work, especially if the floor is hard.

The leg crossover is a floor exercise that integrates dynamic balance and core strength. Begin by sitting on the ground with your legs out straight. Place your hands on the ground behind you for balance support. Keep your back straight and lean back to a 45-degree angle. Raise your legs off the ground until your toes are roughly elbow height. Extend both legs out into a wide V shape. Then bring them together and cross your left leg over your right. Return to the wide V, then cross your right leg over your left. Repeat the exercise ten to 12 times, alternating the leg on top.

The exercise should strengthen the superficial and deep core muscles in the abdomen, back, and sides of the torso, as well as the abductor muscles on the outside of the hips and the adductor muscles on the inside of the thighs. These muscles work to keep the torso from rocking side to side or slumping backward during the repetitions. To increase the difficulty of the exercise, lift your hands off the ground.

BASES OF SUPPORT

There are many ways to change the body's base of support. Some of them occur during everyday actions like kneeling to pick up a dropped item or sitting in a chair. Athletes change their bases of support in more dramatic ways. Gymnasts performing cartwheels are changing their support bases to their hands. Ballet dancers often rely on their toes as bases of support.

Side planks can be done as either a static or a dynamic exercise.

Side planks with a dip can improve balance on the sides of the body. This exercise works many core muscles, especially the obliques along the sides of the torso. Begin by lying on one side. Prop up your upper body on your forearm, with your elbow directly under your shoulder. Be sure not to sink into this shoulder, though. Place your other arm somewhere off the ground, such as on top of your hip or folded in front of your chest.

Stack your feet on top of each other and push into your forearm to raise your hips from the ground. Keeping your body straight and facing forward, lower your hip down to the ground and then lift it back up. Engage your abdominal muscles and squeeze your glutes to keep your body stable during the dipping motion. Repeat ten to 15 times on each side. If the exercise is too difficult, support yourself with your knees rather than your feet.

The single-leg bridge is another good core exercise. It improves core stability and strengthens abdominal, back, glutes, hamstring, and hip muscles. Begin the single-leg bridge by lying on your back with your knees bent and feet on the ground. Raise one leg from the ground and extend it straight forward. Push into the leg on the ground and raise your hips, holding your body in a straight, slanted line that runs through the knees, hips, and shoulders.

Engage your abdominal muscles and glutes to help keep your back straight and your torso strong and steady. Avoid arching or rounding your back. Your hips should be level; one should not tilt lower than the other. After pushing up, lower your hips in a slow, controlled movement. Perform the exercise 15 times on each leg.

Bridges can be done with one or two legs on the ground. Balancing with one leg through the movement works the core.

ESSENTIAL FACTS

What Is Stretching and Balance?

- Stretching exercises use certain movements and positions to lengthen muscles.
- Balance is the ability to maintain upright posture and stability.
- There are two main types of stretching and balance exercise: static and dynamic. Static exercises involve stillness. Dynamic exercises involve controlled movement.
- Stretching and balance practice can be stand-alone routines or incorporated into other exercise routines.
- Stretching and balance are used in general health and wellness programs, athletic training, rehabilitation, and management of chronic health conditions.

Benefits of Stretching and Balance

- Relieves muscle tension.
- Increases blood flow.
- Encourages a healthy range of motion in the joints.
- Promotes flexibility, strength, power, muscle endurance, and recovery.
- Makes the movements of both sports and everyday life easier and safer.
- Reduces stress and activates the body systems responsible for rest and relaxation.
- Activates muscles and improves communication between the brain, muscles, and senses.

Quote

"To really reap the benefits of exercise, you need to add flexibility and balance training to the mix."

—American Academy of Orthopaedic Surgeons

GLOSSARY

abdominal

Relating to the band of muscles that lines the walls of the trunk of the body.

aerobic

Physical exercise that uses oxygen to power the heart and muscles.

BOSU ball

An exercise tool with a rubbery inflated dome on one side and a flat platform on the other.

cardiovascular

Related to the heart and blood vessels.

core

Muscles that stabilize the midsection of the body, including abdominal and back muscles.

hormone

A chemical produced by the body that creates different effects throughout the body.

kinesiology

The study of human body movement.

ligament

A fibrous tissue that connects bones.

musculoskeletal system

The system of bones, muscles, and their connective tissues.

physiology

A branch of biology that focuses on body functions.

plyometric

Relating to exercises involving quick stretching and contracting of muscles, such as jumps.

range of motion

The extent to which a joint or muscle can move.

recovery

The time between exercise sessions when the body adapts to training.

resistance

An opposing force a person uses to exercise muscles to increase muscle strength.

set

A collection of reps.

skeletal muscle

A muscle attached to bone.

tendon

A cord of tissue that connects muscle to bone.

ADDITIONAL RESOURCES

Selected Bibliography

Behm, David G. *The Science and Physiology of Flexibility and Stretching*. Routledge Taylor & Francis, 2019.

Faigenbaum, Avery D., Rhodri S. Lloyd, and Jon L. Oliver. *Essentials of Youth Fitness*. Human Kinetics, 2020.

Nelson, Arnold G., and Jouko Kokkonen. *Stretching Anatomy*. 3rd ed., Human Kinetics, 2020.

Further Readings

Allman, Toney. *Living a Healthy Lifestyle*. ReferencePoint, 2020.

Hayes, Kevin, editor. *Fitness Information for Teens*. 5th ed., Omnigraphics, 2021.

Huddleston, Emma. *Nutrition and Exercise*. Abdo, 2021.

Online Resources

To learn more about stretching and balance, please visit **abdobooklinks.com** or scan this QR code. These links are routinely monitored and updated to provide the most current information available.

More Information

For more information on this subject, contact or visit the following organizations:

Fit Kids Foundation

1143 Crane St., Unit 203
Menlo Park, CA 94025
fitkids.org

Fit Kids is a nonprofit organization that designs movement and mindfulness programs for schools and communities. It provides information about the health benefits of fitness and free exercise videos on its website.

Human Kinetics

1607 N. Market St.
Champaign, IL 61820
us.humankinetics.com

Human Kinetics produces textbooks, educational programs, digital material, and other information on exercise, nutrition, and health. It offers information for professionals and for students.

Penn State Department of Kinesiology

Pennsylvania State University
276 Recreation Bldg.
University Park, PA 16802
hhd.psu.edu/kines

This department at Pennsylvania State University studies human movement and its role in people's lives. It has a Center for Fitness and Wellness, and it sponsors "Exercise Is Medicine" events, including stretching and mindfulness activities.

SOURCE NOTES

Chapter 1. Stretching and Destressing

1. "Health Benefits of Exercise." *Jump Start by WebMD*, n.d., webmd.com. Accessed 26 Jan. 2024.

2. April Fulton. "Virtual Workouts Spiked during the Pandemic—and the Trend Is Sticking Around." *NPR*, 22 May 2022, npr.org. Accessed 26 Jan. 2024.

Chapter 2. What Is Stretching and Balance?

1. Phil Page. "Current Concepts in Muscle Stretching for Exercise and Rehabilitation." *International Journal of Sports Physical Therapy*, vol. 7, no. 1, Feb. 2012, ncbi.nlm.nih.gov. Accessed 12 Feb. 2024.

2. Amy Crawford. "Good Science Changes: That's a Good Thing." *University of Michigan School of Public Health*, 14 May 2021, sph.mich.edu. Accessed 26 Jan. 2024.

3. Jenny Marder. "For a Stable, Strong Core, Forget about Crunches." *New York Times*, 8 Feb. 2023, nytimes.com. Accessed 26 Jan. 2024.

4. Christie Matheson. "Strengthening and Protecting Your Core Muscles." *New York University Langone Health*, 2013, froemkelab.med.nyu.edu. Accessed 26 Jan. 2024.

Chapter 3. Stretching and Balance and the Body

1. Barbara J. Campbell. "Exercise and Bone Health." *American Academy of Orthopedic Surgeons*, n.d., orthoinfo.aaos.org. Accessed 26 Jan. 2024.

2. L'Oreal Thompson Payton. "The Mental and Physical Benefits of Stretching: What This Essential Part of Your Workout Does for Your Brain and Body." *Fortune*, 6 Jan. 2023, fortune.com. Accessed 6 Mar. 2024.

3. "Balance Issues." *Cleveland Clinic*, n.d., my.clevelandclinic.org. Accessed 26 Jan. 2024.

4. "Introduction to the Muscular System." *National Cancer Institute*, n.d., training.seer.cancer.gov. Accessed 26 Jan. 2024.

Chapter 4. Static Stretching

1. Mary L. Gavin. "Stretching." *Kids Health*, Mar. 2022, kidshealth.org. Accessed 12 Feb. 2024.

2. "Stretches for the Back, Shoulders, and Arms." *Harris County University of Georgia Extension Office*, n.d., extension.uga.edu. Accessed 26 Jan. 2024.

3. "Should You Lock Your Joints When You Stretch?" *International Sports Sciences Association*, 15 Aug. 2015, issaonline.com. Accessed 26 Jan. 2024.

4. "Stretches for the Back, Shoulders, and Arms." *University of Georgia*, n.d., extension.uga.edu. Accessed 12 Feb. 2024.

5. "All That Texting and Scrolling Leads to a Rise in 'Tech Neck.'" *University of Texas Southwestern Medical Center*, 14 Feb. 2023, utsouthwestern.edu. Accessed 26 Jan. 2024.

SOURCE NOTES CONTINUED

Chapter 5. Dynamic Stretching

1. "Stretch It Out with Dynamic Stretching." *Children's Mercy Kansas City*, 3 May 2019, news.childrensmercy.org. Accessed 26 Jan. 2024.

2. "Understanding the Difference between Dynamic and Static Stretching." *Cleveland Clinic*, 28 May 2020, health.clevelandclinic.org. Accessed 12 Feb. 2024.

Chapter 6. Static Balance

1. Paige Waehner. "Stabilizer Muscles Used in Exercise and for Balance." *Verywell Fit*, 19 Apr. 2022, verywellfit.com. Accessed 12 Feb. 2024.

2. Gill Connell. "Why Hopscotch Matters." *Moving Smart*, n.d., movingsmartblog.com. Accesssed 14 Mar. 2024.

3. Tyler Allen. "Balancing Act: Progressions of Static and Dynamic Balance." *Strive Physiotherapy & Performance*, n.d., strivept.ca. Accessed 12 Feb. 2024.

4. Jim Carpentier. "11 Kneeling Exercises for Strength and Core Stability." *Stack*, 28 Oct. 2017, stack.com. Accessed 26 Jan. 2024.

5. Per Welinder and Peter Whitley. *Mastering Skateboarding*. Human Kinetics, 2011.

Chapter 7. Dynamic Balance

1. Shriya Maharaj. "Static Balance vs. Dynamic Balance Exercises." *Propel Physiotherapy*, n.d., propelphysiotherapy.com. Accessed 26 Jan. 2024.

2. Chris Freytag. "5 Balance Exercises to Boost Stability and Performance." *Verywell Fit*, 5 Oct. 2022, verywellfit.com. Accessed 26 Jan. 2024.

INDEX

ABOUT THE AUTHOR

Rebecca Morris

Rebecca Morris is the author of several nonfiction books for students. She has degrees in English, international relations, and comparative humanities. She enjoys taking exercise classes and running.